I0687751

OSCAR & ALICE

oddfeathercreative.co
@jemofthebrew

Published by Oddfeather Creative 2021
Copyright © Jemimah Brewster 2021

The moral right of Jemimah Brewster to be identified as the author of this
work has been asserted by her in
accordance with the Copyright Act of 1968.
All rights reserved. No part of this book may be reproduced in any manner
whatsoever without written permission except in the case of brief
quotations embodied in critical articles and reviews.

For permission requests, email the publisher
at oddfeathercreative@gmail.com

Cover and illustrations designed by Alex E Clark @lexlotl

ISBN: 978-0-6452807-1-5

First published 2021

A catalogue record for this
book is available from the
National Library of Australia

The characters in this book are fictitious and any resemblance to
real persons, living or dead, is coincidental.

Oscar & Alice

A suburban Gothic novella

JEMIMAH BREWSTER

Oddfeather Creative

CONTENTS

I

Morte & Mortality

II

Vanstone & Stoned

III

Caring & Covens

IV

Absence & Absolution

V

Death & Departure

ACKNOWLEDGEMENTS
61
ABOUT THE AUTHOR
62

Part I:
Morte &
Mortality

I

Morte & Mortality

Meet Alice Morte. Her family name means 'death', and since last October death is all she's been able to think about. Her twin brother, Oscar Morte, was struck by lightning while standing on the roof of the Morte family home at number four Yardley Court, the last house in the cul-de-sac. The force of the strike flung Oscar from the roof into the middle of the Court, although he was definitely dead before he hit the road. At least, that's what the official report stated after the police investigated the matter.

At first no one realised that it was Oscar lying charred and smoking in the middle of the cul-de-sac, because, despite an extensive search later that evening, his head was nowhere to be found. Again, the official report came to the rescue, stating that the force of the lightning strike had incinerated Oscar's cranium, leaving only the brittle, gaping sinew of his neck. This was also, it posited, evidence to support the fact that he died instantly.

This was small comfort to his mother, Fenella Morte, who was, in a word, hysterical when the body was discovered, and Oscar's disappearance noted, and the two events put together as one. She flung herself bodily onto the tarmac of the cul-de-sac, wailing and keening with woe. Len Morte, Oscar's father, was more stoic, in line with his lifelong tendency of not showing much emotion. Neither Len nor Fenella had prior records of violence, aggression or abuse; disappointing suspects at best. Although the police would have preferred to pin the incident on a determined perpetrator, the best they could hope for was criminal negligence. However, due to the general strangeness and impracticality of the boy's death, they were unable to blame it on anyone in particular.

Alice was not questioned regarding the incident, which was ruled an accident for want of evidence as anything else. Or, to be more accurate, it was attributed to an 'act of God'. It was fortunate that Alice was never investigated because, although she had nothing whatsoever to do with her brother's grisly demise, the Morte twins did not get along. In fact, they rather vehemently did not get on, and Alice was unable to hide her deep and abiding contempt for her twin, even in death.

From a young age Alice had shown a predilection for the darker and more mystical side of life. She collected bones and kept them in a box in the greenhouse that was attached to the side of the Morte home. She believed in ghosts, angels, witches, and spirits. She fed the stray cats that slunk around the forest behind their house at twilight. She read books about teens who slayed monsters and sometimes fell in love with them. And she fervently eschewed anything that her mother wanted her to do or wear because it was more 'likeable' and 'attractive'.

Alice pursued her interest in death, nature, and fiction with pre-teen fervor, and made the grave – as it turned out – mistake of sharing these interests with Oscar one holidays before the school year started. Oscar, doted on by his mother and favoured by teachers and classmates for his larrikin brashness and cherubim curls, took it upon himself to correct Alice's interests by educating her about 're-ality'. Because in his world there was nothing that could not be ra-tionalised or controlled, including her. Soon, facts, logic, and science were the only things that interested Oscar, at school and at home. At meal times he would admonish his father for saying things like, 'I'm so full I could burst!', by retorting, 'That's illogical. Humans only burst if they're a rotting corpse. Are you a rotting corpse?'

Fenella bought him a chemistry set and organised after-school tu-tors in mathematics, coding, and robotics. In her rose-tinted vision of the future her handsome, rational son was a Zuckerberg, a Musk, a Jobs – destined for riches and prestige with his vast intellect and razor-sharp judgement. But Oscar really didn't care about logic or learning or science. His interest was purely to counter Alice's. What he really wanted was to prove her wrong, whatever she was doing.

So Alice spent her days reading fantasy novels, dying her hair black and wearing striped tights, caring for animals and collecting their eventual skeletons. And he spent his days cheating at science competitions and trapping and killing small creatures, then experi-menting on them in increasingly grotesque ways. After reading the abridged, children's version of *Frankenstein's Monster* he became con-vinced that if he reanimated a dead body he could prove that God did not exist; man could take and give life at will, and thus achieve fame and fortune for himself. It would also, most importantly, cement his status as dominant over his sister once and for all, because he could manipulate and control the 'real' world that had served him so well.

Thus, if the police had questioned Alice about Oscar's death, she might have said something along the lines of, 'My brother insisted on living in the real world and it burned him alive,' and then been sent to a psychologist whom she would have treated terribly. But she was not questioned, because how could a teenage girl wield the kind of power that could spontaneously blow a person's head off? That power, it seemed, was only in the domain of nature and God.

*

Fenella Morte was, as previously noted, hysterical at her son's demise. Although entirely warranted, her hectic displays of grief plagued the other occupants of number four Yardley Court for the next six months. In that time, two other events occurred in the cul-de-sac that, in the end, were the proverbial straws that broke the camel's back. The camel, in this instance, being Fenella Morte.

The first event appeared, at the time, to impact Len Morte more than his wife, although it did negatively affect all three of the re-maining Mortes at number four. The drain in the curb directly in front of their house flooded. A downpour of biblical proportions had battered their little neighbourhood for most of the day. When it fi-nally abated and the sun shone through the thinning clouds in the evening the drain was deeply flooded, including the footpath, verge, and road in the top half-moon of the cul-de-sac. And it was not just floodwater. It became obvious, as the sun cast delicious peaches, golds and rose pinks across the lawn, that sewage was mixed in with the water that refused to drain away, creating an almost visible haze of smell that apparently emanated from the house itself.

For the evening it was merely inconvenient, but it had barely drained the following morning, and by the next evening, a Sunday, Fenella had badgered Len into calling their local MP to get it fixed. This may have been a slight overreaction, and the MP, whose per-sonal number Fenella acquired through her own wily means, took it somewhat personally that he was being bothered with such a minor matter on a Sunday evening. He then told his team, as well as the council workers who would generally have cleared such a blockage, not to attend to it. This, also, was something of an overreaction, and

Fenella's reaction to this overreaction was sharply felt throughout the household.

The second event, and the final camel-collapsing straw, was the fire.

A pernicious and entirely false rumour had pervaded the neighbourhood following Oscar's death, implying that he had died of negligence as a result of poor parenting. This rumour had been started by the Morte's neighbour, Jackie Peach, at number two Yardley Court, although she would have absolutely no idea how her various comments, implications and intonations had created such a horrid twisting of the truth. Jackie was often forced to deny that her chronic rumour-mongering had anything at all to do with her. How can she be blamed if others choose to leap to and believe such terrible things, and then pass them on to their friends, and their friends' friends (and all of their hairdressers)?

The vicious buzzings of this rumour finally manifested several months after Oscar's death in a flaming bag of faeces with 'Shit for shit parents' written on it (although the presence of the flames rendered this literary masterpiece ultimately unreadable, more's the pity), left on the Morte's front doorstep. Unfortunately for the pranksters and, more importantly, the remaining Mortes, no one was home at the time of the delivery. An unusually warm autumn wind had fanned the flames of the bag and, along with the straw doormat and greasy diet of the defecator, the flames licked higher and higher. They blistered and scarred the varnished wood of the front door, expanding and curling the wooden door frame, and heating and flaking the metal of the porch roof. The fire made its way into the bush beside the front step and climbed up to the kitchen window before Edith, their neighbour at number six Yardley Court, noticed and put it out.

Alice arrived home first that day and entered number four via the greenhouse at the side of the house with music in her ears, as she did every day after school. Len then arrived home, parking his van around the back of the house in the garage, as he did every Friday evening. So it was Fenella, returning from a very extended lunch with some friends, who first noticed the charred front door. Again she badgered Len to call someone, this time their home insurance provider, who promised to send an agent to assess the damage as soon as possible. Fenella then badgered Len to call the police, before realising that another burn-related event so soon after Oscar's death would look very suspicious, further fuelling the rumours of their negligence.

The insurance inspector arrived two weeks after the fact, completed a quick assessment, and pronounced that, as the damage was not structural and the dwelling was still secure and liveable, the company would not cover the cost of fixing it without a significant up-front payment. Fenella, irritated but not surprised, placed responsibility for fixing the burns firmly – and loudly – on Len, and left it at that.

Except that Len, having recently lost his son, mocked by the flooded drain and pervasive smell of sewage, and now the scarring of the front of his house by persons unknown, had no strength left to replace the damaged porch. Although he was unable to articulate it, the charred front of his home became a manifestation of his soul: damaged, scarred, broken. So he did not fix it, and that is why his wife left.

*

Fenella Morte left number four Yardley Court on a crisp morning in early April without a word of warning or farewell to her teenage daughter or disconsolate husband. Several days after her departure they received a brief, businesslike letter explaining that she was gone (as if they had not noticed) and that she would send a courier to collect her things, which were packed in boxes in the greenhouse. Alice and Len, upon reading the letter in the kitchen, both glanced through the side laundry door into the greenhouse and finally noticed the moving boxes and suitcases that had been there for several days. Oscar's belongings, including his two bicycles, unopened science magazines, sports equipment, and Oulie's kennel, were also stacked against the greenhouse walls. Neither father nor daughter took much notice of what was in there, as they both considered it exclusively a thoroughfare and the territory of Oulie.

Oscar had whined for and received Oulie, a boisterous golden retriever, on his eleventh birthday. Alice had also whined for a cat for the same birthday, and had been told that little boys need a man's-best-friend, that dogs are useful and cats are not, and instead she was given a subscription to a pre-teen magazine. Oscar had looked after his new puppy for exactly one week, during which time the poor animal irreversibly imprinted on him, and then was left to live out in the greenhouse to be fed intermittently by whichever family member remembered to do it, least of all Oscar. Oulie was let out into the back yard to run around and frequently escaped into the forest behind the cul-de-sac where he had no self-control, terrorising nearby fields of sheep and horses, always returning home again before being caught.

Oulie had been much quieter since his master died, his large brown eyes sorrowful, whining outside Oscar's room. He had also taken to digging frantically in the garden near where Oscar fell. Alice soon took pity on the poor animal and began taking care of him, letting him sleep on her bed and feeding him from her dinner plate. She was pleased to have Oulie's company when Fenella left, although she could never admit to herself that she enjoyed a dog's company so much. Dogs were not very mysterious, nor mystical, nor intelligent. Or at least, Oulie wasn't very intelligent. Mainly he was just too wholesome for a girl like her, and with her ambitions to enter her school's Witch Guild, she needed to be more edgy, not less.

*

Alice discovered the existence of the Witches' Guild before Oscar died, but her tendency towards non-participation, loner aesthetic, and general social anxiety had put her off trying to join. But, just after the fire that scarred the front of the Morte house, Alice had started to hear things. If Fenella were still around she may have tried to speak to her about it. But her mother had left, betraying her daughter by being entirely absent, and Alice was left with more than the usual burden of teen angst and now a disembodied voice in her head.

At first it was barely a whisper, hardly louder than the wind outside, and she pretended it was her imagination. It only happened in the cul-de-sac, so for the first time school became a relief more than a torment. But as the days passed the voice grew stronger and more insistent, and Alice's worst fears were confirmed when she knew beyond a doubt that it was Oscar speaking to her. One night she awoke in the wee hours and the whispering was clearer than ever.

My head, it hurts, it's gone, find it, my head is gone, I need my head...

Alice sat up in bed.

'Oscar?'

My head, it hurts, I need it, please...

'Oscar is that you?'

I want my head, I need to go, you need to find it, I can't stay...

'How can you speak if your head is missing?'

Don't try and be clever! You stupid, idiot girl.

'Oh I suppose you don't need my help then, if I'm such an idiot!'

No, please! I need my head, I can't leave without it, please Allie, I need to go...

Alice frowned in the darkness, whispering, 'Alright I'll find your stupid head, but only so you're properly gone.'

Ok, thank you, I need it, don't forget...

Drifting back to sleep Alice wondered what to do. Oscar's head had been disintegrated by the forces of nature (or God), so how was she going to find any of it? And when she did, what would she do with it? She drifted off, her mind full of troubled thoughts, and soon she started to dream. In the dream she was surrounded by friends who understood this kind of thing, how to work with dead things, how to find lost things, and how to move spirits on to the other side. By the time she was fully asleep a plan had formed, a plan just strange enough that it might work.

*

The next day she approached Chelsea Woodward before their geography class, summoned every ounce of her courage, and said, 'Chelsea. Hi. I'm Alice. I'd like to join the Guild.'

Chelsea gave her a look of adolescent contempt. 'What Guild? Who even are you?'

'I'm Alice. Alice Morte. I mean the' – she whispered - 'Witches' Guild.'

Chelsea's eyes widened slightly, and one of her friends leaned toward her and whispered, 'That's Oscar Morte's freaky sister.'

Chelsea and her sidekick regarded Alice, crossing their arms to raise the stakes just a bit higher.

'Alright. You can join the Witches' Guild.'

'Oh wow, really? That would be great because I have a problem-'

'But not before you run the trial.'

'The... trial?'

'The trial of Witches.'

'Like, I have to jump in a pond and not float?'

'What? What are you even talking about, no! You need to complete some tasks for me. For us. The Guild. And then you can join.'

'Oh, ok. What do I need to do?'

Chelsea and her friend had a hurried conversation behind their hands, then turned back to Alice.

'You need to get us some witches' hair.'

'Witches-? Is that like a plant or something?'

'No, you idiot. A handful of hair, from a witch. Not one of us, obviously, but a different witch. Preferably an adult.'

'Uhh. I don't know any other witches, just you guys.'

Chelsea smiled unpleasantly. 'Well I guess you can't be in the Guild then.'

They entered the classroom for geography, sitting with the rest of their coven in the back of the class. Alice took her usual seat at the front – all the easier for coming and going quickly – and pondered what to do.

It was the next morning in her advanced English Lit class that Alice had a breakthrough. Miss Greenhaven, mistress of the literary novel and wearer of gorgeous outfits that were wasted on her students, was wearing a pentagram necklace. Alice was no expert on witches, but she knew the pentagram was generally witchy, along with ankhs and crystals and black cats. She watched Miss Greenhaven closely for the rest of the lesson and approached her after class.

'Miss? I just wanted to say that I-I really like your necklace.'

'Oh? Thank you.'

'It, um. Is it for anything?'

'Decoration.'

'I mean, is it significant? You know, in your line of work.'

'Only as an unfortunate conversation-starter with students.'

'Oh. Ok... so you're not, like, a witch?'

Miss Greenhaven was a seasoned English teacher in her mid-thirties and had been in the public school system her entire professional life, so she had a very good poker face. But she wasn't made of actual stone, so she snorted with laughter. Alice looked hurt.

'A witch? Did studying Macbeth make you think I like to spy and curse and pull people's strings for nefarious schemes? Don't be silly.'

Alice looked at the floor, crestfallen. Miss Greenhaven relented. 'Well I suppose it's not that far from the truth.'

Alice's face was strained, but she looked up at Miss Greenhaven through the strands of greasy black hair that perpetually fell in her face, and said in a fierce but shaking whisper:

'I need to find a witch, an adult witch. It's... for a trial. I have to join the Witches' Guild.'

'The Witches' what?'

'Guild. Chelsea Woodward and some others. I heard some people talking about it last year and I think that... I think they can help me. So I need to join.'

Miss Greenhaven put a hand on her hip, her face sceptical.

'Chelsea Woodward, huh? And what's the trial?'

'I need...' Alice gulped, 'I need a handful of hair, from a witch. Not one of them. Obviously. A different witch.'

'So you want to know if I'm a witch so that you can take a handful of my hair to a group of girls to become part of their club?'

Alice looked at the floor and mumbled an affirmative.

Miss Greenhaven looked at her contemptuously, but she felt a bit sorry for Alice and her contempt was not at full strength.

'Why on earth do you want to be part of any club that contains Chelsea Woodward? Why don't you join the basketball lunch games or the chess club or take up planking or literally anything else?'

'It's the witches. I... it's my brother. I need their help, because of him.'

Alice, despite her staunch anger at everything, and teachers in particular, was under-slept and vulnerable, and was beginning to deeply regret this entire plan. Miss Greenhaven had of course known Oscar and knew what had happened to him, and she softened a little more.

'Well Alice, let's say that I am a witch. I don't want to give you a handful of my hair, for obvious reasons, so you won't be able to join Chelsea's club.'

'Guild.'

'Whatever. But as a witch I can help you with your brother. I may enlist the help of other fellow witches as well. Mrs Hughes is a witch, although you should never ask her about it. Also Hayley, who's in on Thursdays and Fridays. We can make our own club. Coven. And between us all I'm sure we can help you with your brother.'

Alice knew full well that Hayley was a school psychologist, and that Mrs Hughes the principal was definitely not a witch (what self-respecting purveyor of the dark arts would become a school principal?), but she had a terrible feeling that Chelsea's 'Guild' was just a front for wearing black and excluding people, like Alice.

'Ok. I won't take your hair. As the first act of our newly-created coven I need an extension on the Blake essay.'

Miss Greenhaven executed her best glare at Alice, but didn't say anything, and Alice walked away before she changed her mind about any of it. She wouldn't tell her teacher about the voice, but she was sure that someone would have an idea of how to find Oscar's head. Or at least how to gather the pieces.

*

'Len, sweetie! Coo-ee, Len! Over here, darling!'

Len Morte had spent the day up to his elbows in blocked laundry sinks, too-narrow toilet pipes, gunk-filled dishwasher drains, and grass-clogged downpipes. He had returned home to number four

Yardley Court to discover that the drain in front of their house was even more flooded, and it was feeling more and more like a personal affront. Unblocking drains was his stock-in-trade; ensuring that water and waste moved from one location smoothly to another without interruption, blockage or leaks. His work was a small but vital part of civilisation. Ever since the Romans and their ill-conceived lead pipes, all the way to Bazalgette's sewers under London that ultimately ended the Great Stink of 1858, the work of a plumber was invisible but essential, only noticeable by its absence. And he liked it that way, to fly under the radar, but know that someone in his line of work was needed by every single person in the country.

And yet, the drain in front of his house was blocked and there was nothing he could do about it. He could unclog, drain and fix systems in any building he entered, but he could not fix the drain in front of his own home. Multiple calls to the city council had resulted in dismissals and waiting lists. In any other situation he would simply wade into the quagmire and unblock it himself, but, having already caused so much fuss about it, the council would know that it was he who fixed it and he knew from experience that they were not kind in dealing with those who took civil works matter into their own hands. And, more pertinently, he was developing a sort of mental block in relation to the upkeep of his own home. Oscar's death had laid a blanket of deepest sorrow on his shoulders, and Fenella's absence had only added to the weight of it. He wasn't an expressive man before, but he now wore a mask of indifference that rendered his expression permanently unchanged, because if it did, he would crack and weep and he would never stop.

But that did not deter Jackie Peach.

'Over here! By the vine! Coo-ee, Len!'

He looked around and finally spotted his perky neighbour's rampantly made-up face peering over the fence by the passionfruit vine.

'Jackie. How goes it?'

'Oh, you poor darling man, I've been trying to reach you for weeks! I am so terribly sorry to hear that Fenella left, she was such a dear! We had the most wonderful conversations, often in this exact spot! You must be absolutely heartbroken that she's gone, you were so terribly happy together! And so soon after Oscar's death! How's little Alice holding up? And more importantly, how are you? You poor, handsome man. I'd like to bake you a pie and feed it to you, make everything better! You must come over for dinner this week. No I won't take no for an answer. This Wednesday, come over at six, bring little Alice if she's around, and I'll make my delicious beef pot pie for dinner. You'll love it. And then you can have peaches for dessert!' She winked slowly, and he stared at her, his expression the same as ever.

'Sounds alright. Thanks.'

Jackie smiled even more broadly, clasping her hands together.

'Wonderful! What a treat it will be to have you. Although I'm sure Alice will have her own plans. Teens are always off with each other, tick-tocking and retro gramming and so on, so no need to bother her. It can be just you and me! Oh, I'm so looking forward to it, I can't wait to crack that nut! Too-roo for now!' She waved heartily as she walked back to her house, as though she were departing on a ship and he was disappearing into the vast distance.

He eyed the vine in front of him and carefully pulled some of the dead leaves and buds off it, pinching the stems rather than ripping them so as not to damage it. Then he went inside via the greenhouse, past Fenella's boxes and Oscar's bicycles, and in through the laundry door.

'Alice! We're going to tea at Jackie's on Wednesday!'

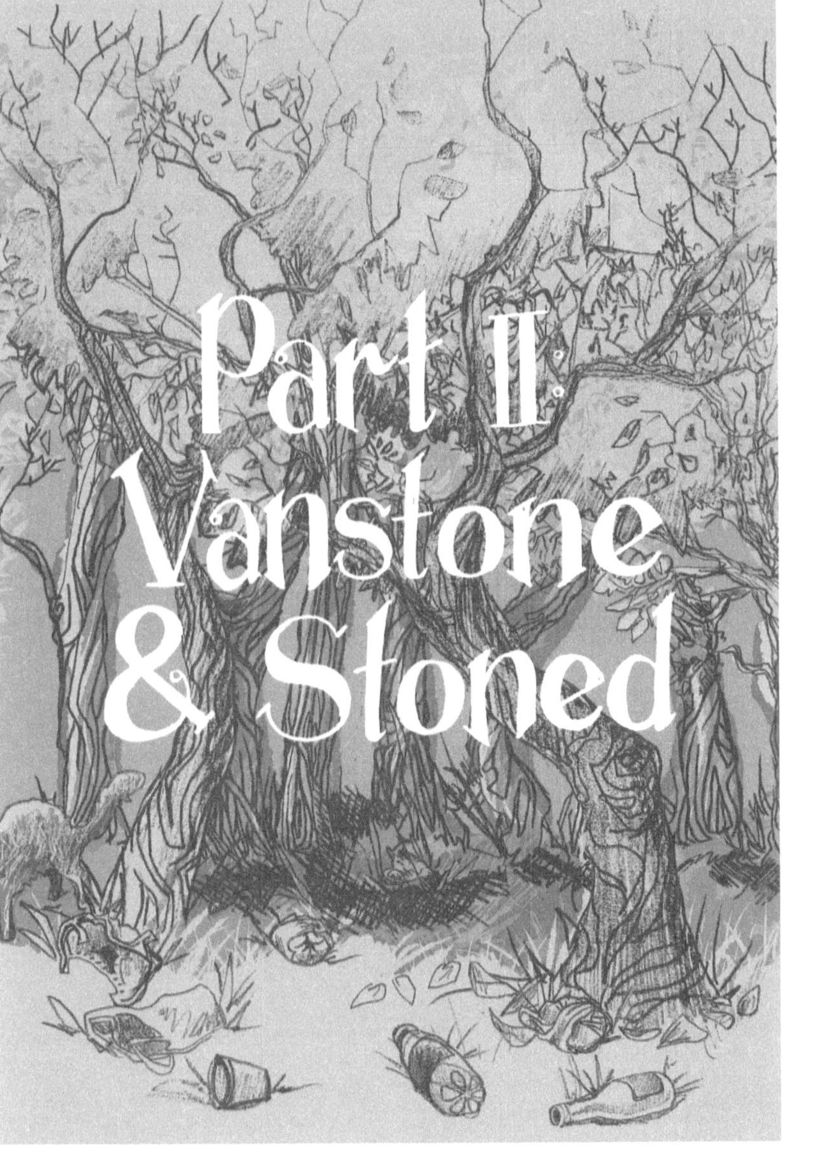
Part II:
Vanstone
& Stoned

II

Vanstone & Stoned

Edith Vanstone lived at number six Yardley Court, to the left of the Morte residence. She told people that she had lived there all her life, that her house was built first, and even made people refer to it as Yardley Manor. But she had lived there not much longer than the Mortes or Jackie Peach when the cul-de-sac was built barely a decade ago. Nevertheless, she carried herself with deportment and did and said much as she pleased. At eighty-six years of age she wanted to get a bit more fun out of life before she got properly old and things really started to go down hill, and seeing the frustration in her carer's eyes as she patiently listened to Edith's entirely fictional semi-royal lineage was the greatest joy the old woman could ask for.

Edith had only one close living relative: her son Derek, who rarely visited. Her carer, Margaret, came twice a week to clean, make sure Edith was taking her pills, and take her into town for shopping and appointments. Edith complained passionately that she did not need a carer and could easily manage all of these tasks herself, and Margaret let her think that because she had worked with the elderly for many years and knew it was vital that they retain their pride, and constant complaining was a necessary symptom of that.

Besides Margaret's visits and Derek's occasional phone call, Edith was left mostly to her own devices, which is precisely how she preferred it. She would go for long walks in the scraggly forest behind the cul-de-sac, and she used to feed the stray cats that sometimes ventured as far as the alley between her house and the Mortes. She stopped feeding them when she saw nine-year-old Alice doing the same thing, deciding to leave that responsibility to the strange black-clad, book-carrying little girl next door. And that was the beginning of her soft spot for Alice, and her interest in the Morte family as a source of entertainment.

From her upstairs windows Edith could look out into the cul-de-sac and see clearly into the upstairs windows of the Morte residence, where Alice and Oscar's rooms were situated. She could also see into the greenhouse that Len had built during the summer Oscar and Alice turned five, which extended off the entire ground-floor side of the house closest to Edith's. It was from her upstairs study, looking through the window that gave the best view of the Morte's home, that Edith had witnessed Oscar's death, although she hadn't realised it at the time. It had been after a long walk to tend to her lettuce patch, and she most certainly had not returned sober.

Edith's long walks in the forest behind the cul-de-sac were not solely for fresh air. Eighty-six-year-old Edith Vanstone had learned as a young adult, when her husband left her for his secretary and she was forced to make ends meet with a baby and no marketable skills, to cultivate what she rather coyly referred to as devil's lettuce. Like many before her, Edith had discovered that discretion, practicality, and a moderately green thumb were all that was needed to grow a small crop, process it, and sell it on for just enough money to keep oneself afloat. She held no particular views about the morality of it, and had only grown it until she had a steadier income that would take care of herself and Derek, so it had been many years since she had even thought of it. But life can be long and age is a constant adversary, so when she moved closer to the equator because the cold was making her joints ache, she specifically chose a house that was near a secluded, wooded area, perfect for hiding a small patch. She could have grown it in her back yard, but her innate pragmatism told her that neighbours tend to be nosy, no matter how clearly you imply your desire for privacy. And she was also deeply suspicious of Margaret, and indeed any carer who was assigned to her, so she took the added precaution of stashing her smoking paraphernalia inside a metal tin under an old log, like a mischievous adolescent.

So Edith had been under the influence of her crop when she returned to number six Yardley Court that day in October, snorting giddily with dry laughter at the sheer volume of discarded nappies, bottles and cigarette butts on the various paths through the forest, as though there weren't enough rubbish dumps everywhere else. She had climbed upstairs and settled into her armchair for a nap, facing into the window to enjoy the cool afternoon breeze. Not long after nodding off, she had woken to the sound of thunder, a storm brewing in the hazy afternoon. Then the figure atop the roof next to hers thrust something into the air and she wondered if her eyesight was getting worse or if that was really a person holding a metal rod. She knew she must be dreaming when the figure emitted a stream of light and flew through the air onto the tarmac of the cul-de-sac, landing top-first with a sickening crunch. She rubbed her eyes roughly, then pulled herself out of the study and into her bed for a proper sleep.

She awoke later that evening to red and blue lights flashing across her bedroom ceiling, and it was then that she fuzzily wondered if it had really been a dream. From the window in her bedroom she saw three police cars and an ambulance parked around the periphery of the cul-de-sac, a loose group of people standing about on the road. She watched for several minutes, wiping her glasses feverishly, her throat parched, unable to look away. Eventually the group dissipated, leaving only two, who lifted something on the ground into a bag. She thought back to what she had blearily witnessed during her nap, remembered the figure attracting lightning from the roof of the Morte house. With only a small twinge of guilt she hoped it was not Alice. If one of the twins had to go she preferred it weren't the little girl who fed stray cats.

*

The next day Edith, despite her deep distrust and dislike of her opposite neighbour, called upon Jackie Peach to find out what had happened at the Morte household. Jackie was irritated to be pulled away from a phone call, which Edith could tell also concerned the grisly goings-on at number four, but she was never one to miss an opportunity to tell someone something they didn't know, even a daft old bat like her neighbour.

'Well Mrs Vanstone, it's quite awful. It seems Oscar was on the roof of number four – although heaven knows why any self-respecting parent would let their child do something so dangerous as climbing on their roof – and was somehow electrocuted while up there. The police interviewed us all and of course I was happy to provide what information I could, but it seems as though there's some question of neglect. What a horrid affair. And Len didn't even look upset! Fenella was distraught of course, and if Alice weren't such a pathetic little thing I'd think she might have caused it somehow, the way she sneers and rolls her eyes at everything. They said the only way he could have been mutilated like that was by a ferocious amount of electricity, so the preliminary conclusions according to the coroner (who used to date my cousin's step-sister's hairdresser) is that he was somehow struck by lightning!' Jackie paused for breath at the height of her speech, which sounded a little rehearsed.

Edith adjusted her glasses, making Jackie's skin-tight jeans and low-cut blouse bulge and wobble before her.

'Mutilated you say?'

'Oh yes, that's the most dreadful part! No one realised it was Oscar at first because his head was blown to smithereens! They had to identify him by his fingerprints, although only the left side were still intact. The rest was too charred to use! I got a good look before they covered up the body and the neck was burned and brittle around the throat. Ghastly. Honestly, the Morte parents should be locked up for their negligence, Mrs Vanstone. If you're lucky enough to bring a child into this world your only job is to keep them safe from harm and that's just the end of it!'

Edith glared at her, although the effect was lost as her eye-line was level with Jackie's immensely squashed-up bosom and Jackie was looking into the distance with a hand on her heart and rehearsed melancholy in her eyes.

'Well, when Derek was a boy he got up to all sorts of things, most of which I didn't know about until years-'

'I'm terribly sorry Mrs Vanstone but my phone is ringing and it's probably my vet. Must dash, too-roo!'

She slammed the door shut. Edith gave her the finger through the bubbled glass.

'It's just Edith, you phony twerp.' She hadn't been a 'Mrs' in over fifty years and had told Jackie more than once, but it never stuck.

Edith returned to her house across the cul-de-sac, taking the stairs up to her study. She sat in her armchair in thought for some time, then turned on her Sight.

Ms Edith Vanstone of number six Yardley Court was not just a strange old lady who laughed at other people's rubbish, grew weed, and tormented the few people who visited her; she could also quite accurately read the emotions of others by their auras. Since her early sixties she had become interested in a field of study that her terribly religious parents had forbidden any mention of during her childhood and adolescence, and that she simply hadn't had time for as a young single mother. Then, as she had aged, she was occasionally accused of being a witch, and so she decided to look into it.

At first she was quite disappointed, finding mainly social media accounts dedicated to crystals and artfully-arranged bundles of herbs. But she persevered and soon struck gold, first in the form of erotic witchcraft, then in plant lore and animal familiars, and lastly in contacting the spirit realm. She bought herself a Ouija board and, after much practice, learned to communicate with her now-deceased ex-husband and torment him in the afterlife. She revived her lettuce-growing skills and also cultivated a kitchen garden for other natural remedies and flavours, and her latest realm of interest was learning to use the Sight, which consisted mainly of reading emotional auras. When one lived to be as richly matured as herself, one began to see patterns in the world, in history, in the peaks, lows and plateaus of daily life, and particularly in the people one meets. Edith's Sight started as observing, cataloguing, remembering, and imagining everything that happened around her, and as a lifelong loner and oddball this all came quite easily. Seeing and reading auras, however, took more practice. Edith had decided early on in life that people were all generally the same and thus treated them with similar levels of contempt and dismissal. She had to unlearn this attitude and teach herself to see others as individuals, as unique beings worthy of her time and attention, rather than fetid rodents who got in her way.

So it was with some surprise that evening, when she accessed her Sight, that she discovered nearby... a fetid rodent.

The experiment Oscar had been attempting when he climbed onto the Morte's roof had been thoroughly debunked by modern science, but the hubris of an indulged teenage boy knows no bounds, not even the boundaries of logic and truth by which Oscar proclaimed to live his life. He had killed a mouse in the back yard and was trying to reanimate it with the power of lightning. Using the same principle, he could simply have used the socket in his bedroom or a car battery and jumper leads, but this would not have achieved the dramatic effect he was going for. When he was on the cover of *The Wall Street Journal* and *GQ* he wanted a dramatised image of himself holding the metal rod aloft on the roof of his boring, dingy childhood home. That's what scientists of the 21st century really lacked: a sense of style and drama as they tamed the elements, bringing nature to its knees with the ferocity of a determined visionary. These were the thoughts going through his head when lightning burned him alive.

Neither the police, the Mortes, nor anyone else who arrived on the scene later that evening noticed the metal rod that had channelled the elements into Oscar's pubescent body, flung backwards on to the roof tiles and wedged in a gutter. The plastic-coated wire he had attached to the base had disconnected, the frayed end dangling from his windowsill, where it continued into his room to the work table, trailing inside a small cardboard box and ending abruptly with a tiny patch of burned fur. Before the wire had disconnected – as it was far too narrow to carry the voltage Oscar had envisioned – a tiny spark had travelled down it, over the windowsill, across the work table, and into the box where the little mouse lay, dead for several hours. Against all odds, and the reason of science and physiology, that spark had reanimated the little rodent, and it had escaped Oscar's room, terrified and trailing smoke like a damaged Spitfire.

Dazed and horrified to be alive again, the mouse had skittered to the last place it remembered: the Morte's back garden. But Oulic had been there on one of his afternoons out of the greenhouse, so it had escaped through a hole in the fence into the alley between the Morte house and Edith's. Then, pursued by the stray cats that prowled the area, it scuttled into Edith's backyard. When Edith turned on her Sight she immediately sensed that something was alive and should not be. Strange purple-black waves emanated from downstairs and, after a bit of poking around, she found the poor reanimated mouse cowering under her kitchen sink. She gently retrieved it, giving off the comforting energy that true animal-lovers possess, and placed it on her kitchen table with a stale biscuit. The mouse relaxed as it nibbled, and thus was able to be mentally probed.

Edith had not practiced this aspect of the Sight much, but a mouse's mind is quite simple, and the only thing it was thinking about was what Edith wanted to know. She saw a shadowy image of Oscar's leering face as he hit the mouse on the head, felt the pain and terror of it awakening again in his room, and Edith was able to piece together what happened.

'Hmm, how ironic. Well, my little rodent, what will we do with you?'

*

Oscar's disembodied voice had reached Edith in late March, after the first flooding of the drain outside the Morte's house and before the bag of flaming faeces scarred the porch. As she had already spent some time in communication with those on the other side she knew immediately what it was, and was annoyed that her meddling in the otherwise restful afterlife of her late ex-husband had led Oscar's spirit right to her. She contacted him through the official channel – Ouija board – to make sure the voice she was hearing was who she thought it was, then spent a few days pondering what to do.

Frankie the mouse nibbled on a cracker in her hand as she thought it over, sitting in her nightgown in her study overlooking the Morte home. She had seen what happened to Oscar that day, and although it had been blurry and she had been disoriented from her nap (and the lettuce), she was sure his head had still been attached when he landed on the ground. Instead of telling anyone what she had seen, she had simply believed it was a THC-induced dream, or a large clumsy bird, and gone back to sleep. But now it seemed that Oscar was missing a vital part of himself that he required before he could move on, and that was a significant problem. She peered down at the cul-de-sac, visualising the spot where Oscar had landed. There was nowhere else his head could be. Perhaps someone had stolen it?

It was during this pondering that Edith saw a figure duck onto the Morte's porch and leave something on the front step. At first she was pleased, thinking that finally the Mortes were receiving flowers and tributes for their poor dead son, which had been entirely lacking in the weeks following his death, probably due to Jackie's toxic rumour-milling. But her original opinion of people, as fetid rodents, was a more accurate assessment, and she quickly saw that the thing left on the porch was not a bunch of flowers or a casserole, but a bag that was on fire.

She carefully put Frankie in his box and made her way downstairs as fast as her knees could take her. She had no fire extinguisher and there was no hose near the front of the Morte house, nor did she have one in her garden that would reach all that way. Jackie's car was absent which meant that she was not home, it was one in the afternoon so none of the Mortes would be home soon either, and Edith had come out onto the street in nothing but her nightgown without calling anyone for help. She watched the flames licking higher and higher, wandering if she had the strength to cart buckets of water over there to douse the flames. Then, casting around, she spotted a spade next to a freshly dug bed in the Morte front garden. She vaguely remembered Len digging there the previous weekend, leaving a large pile of turned earth. She hurried over, took up a shovelful of dirt, and threw it in the middle of the fire, then another, then another, until her shoulders ached, her lungs wheezed, and she was covered in dust and smoke. But it worked. The dirt she threw against the glowing front door and bubbling window paint slowed the heat enough that the flames died out.

As the glowing coals cooled to grey she looked at her handiwork, suddenly feeling intensely embarrassed. She had watched the Morte's son blasted from the roof without telling anyone what she'd seen. She had passed on the job of feeding the stray cats to Alice without ever having spoken to her. And now she had put out a fire on their front doorstep using their own garden soil, without calling a fire truck, while still in her nightgown and harbouring a message that Oscar's spirit could not move on to the afterlife. Edith was not used to feeling embarrassed and she did not take to it. She used the shovel to move the thrown dirt back into the garden, then stood it back in the garden bed, barely noticing that the shovel hit on something and fell sideways onto the ground. She quickly returned home, showered, and went for a long walk to her lettuce patch.

When she returned that evening, again under the influence of her crop, she saw the remaining Mortes standing around the charred porch and having a heated discussion. She turned on her Sight, out of curiosity, and saw that it was Fenella who was having the heated discussion, in shades of neon yellow, orange and pink, and Len was staring at the porch with his arms crossed, glancing now and again at the patch of overturned dirt that Edith had used to put the fire out. His aura was the usual pale blue, which had only grown paler since Oscar died, with a pulse of navy at the centre every time he glanced at the dirt pile. She then turned her detection on Alice and was interested and impressed to note that Alice's aura was mainly one of mirth. She was standing slouched, her long black hair covering most of her face, the usual striped tights, black boots, and large comfort-able-looking cardigan draped over her entire frame. Edith could not see her face, but Alice's aura told her that she was laughing on the inside, heartily, mightily, and only with a petite soupçon of existen-tial despair. That decided it; she could handle her brother's request. Edith was getting too old for this kind of shit.

Part III
Caring
& Covens

III

Caring & Covens

Alice visited Miss Greenhaven every other day, either coming to her office at lunch or staying behind after class. Miss Greenhaven had been peeved at first, cursing herself for letting a teenager get under her skin after so many years of warily answering sarcasm with sarcasm, clever retorts to every taunt, always ready to spikily defend herself. But Alice did not expect much of her, not conversation or favours or special treatment (beyond that first essay extension, which she suspected may have been a put-on). She simply arrived at Miss Greenhaven's office, ate her lunch quietly while reading a book, and left when the bell rang.

Miss Greenhaven remembered all too well her own days in high school and she would have given anything for the chance to sit quietly in an office, reading and eating her lunch undisturbed. But she had not been so lucky. So, without saying anything to Alice, she stopped locking her office at lunch times so Alice could come in. She then started leaving interesting books for her to find, putting them nonchalantly on the chair that Alice sat in. And eventually, after a drawn-out internal battle, she asked Alice about Oscar.

'When we started this... coven, you said that you had a problem with your brother, but you didn't say what it was.'

Alice looked up from her book, annoyed. She had just got to the part where Lady Macbeth cannot wash the blood off her hand; her favourite of all Shakespeare's gore.

'Oscar is... haunting me.' She folded her book away and watched for Miss Greenhaven's reaction.

'As in, you can't stop thinking about him?'

'Yeah I guess. Whenever I'm at home he's like, there. Haunting me. Telling me to find him.'

'Find him how?'

Alice fidgeted with the corner of Macbeth.

'Like... I guess I'm like haunted by his... grisly demise or whatever. You know his head was missing? It like, exploded or something. I just like, wish I knew what happened to it.'

'His head was missing?'

'Yeah, didn't you know? Everyone was talking about it, when it happened. We had to bury him without his head. Mum didn't want to cremate him, but we couldn't have an open coffin or whatever, so they just stuck him in the ground without his head. It's like, sad.'

Miss Greenhaven sipped her tea. No wonder the girl needed some peace and quiet. A gory story like that would follow her around like a bad smell.

'So the whole witch thing. You think a witch can help you find his head?'

'I guess. I had a dream. I know it sounds stupid, but yeah I had a dream that a bunch of witches would help me find his head, then we buried it with the rest of him and he like ascended or moved on or whatever.'

'Do you often do what your dreams tell you?'

'Well, what else am I gonna do? Mum left 'cos she couldn't handle the front of our house looking dodgy, like fixing that would fix everything else somehow. It doesn't matter my twin brother the self-righteous moron is dead, but it's very important that we can walk in and out of our front door. It's not like I have a million people to talk to about this stuff.'

If Edith had been looking at her aura at that moment she would have seen a smattering of mirth floating over a chasm of self-pity, anger, and grief. Miss Greenhaven, who could not see auras but did speak fluent sarcasm, sensed the turmoil swirling inside Alice. She knew well that teens needed to do things in their own time, but that sometimes they also needed a kick up the arse to get started.

'You know, being haunted by the dead is pretty cool, in a way. Very Shakespearean. But if you can't find Oscar's head, you can't find his head. You can't help him. He'll just have to move on by himself.'

Alice chewed on her half-painted, much-bitten thumbnail.

'Yeah I guess. I thought maybe I could like, look for the bits around the house or whatever. I've already had a look, in the front garden and up on the roof, but it was like six months ago and I couldn't find anything.'

'Well then, you'll just have to ignore the haunting and it'll go away.'

'That's great advice.'

'I'm serious. Find something else to do. Distract yourself, find a project. Let him be dead and you can move on.'

'Mmm.'

Miss Greenhaven thought a moment.

'You know, maybe your dream about witches was more about the friends, the community. Have you thought about joining an after-school club?'

'Duh, that's what the Witches' Guild thing was supposed to help with!'

They stared at each other across Miss Greenhaven's desk.

'Sorry. I know you're like, not trained in this stuff. Helping grieving adolescents or whatever. I like our coven. I think it's way better than hanging out with Chelsea Woodward. She's kind of a bitch. I heard she tripped over an old lady at the shops on the weekend.'

'Ha. Maybe we should curse her.'

Alice smiled, despite herself, and reopened Macbeth.

*

Edith had not learned her craft so that she could use it to cause harm, but that arrogant little so-and-so who tripped her in the shopping centre was going to regret everything she'd ever done up to that moment by the time Edith had finished with her. Oh, she'd protested her innocence, saying, 'Oh my God I'm *so* sorry!' at least a dozen times, but Edith had heard a high-pitched giggle just before she hit the ground, and that hare-brained little streak had a look of triumph on her face that no amount of blasphemous apologies could make up for. Ha, well joke's on her; Edith had snagged a few hairs from the girl when she was helped up and now she was going to cause some damage.

Since she had redirected Oscar's pleas to his still-living sibling, not much had happened over at the Morte's that she could see. She occasionally wondered if she should tell them that she had put out the fire on their porch, but no police ever arrived to investigate, and no one ever came to ask her if she saw anything, so she thought it best to let it lie. Apparently Fenella, the Mrs Morte, had left the residence with no signs of returning, but from the outside there was no change following her departure. The only development, which she watched with an increasing sense of foreboding, was that Jackie Peach had a new habit of being in her front garden every evening at the time that Len arrived home from work, spraying water on the dirt or wielding a shiny trowel as she played on her phone. Jackie's aura suggested, as far as Edith could interpret it, a sort of pent-up-ness, as though she were blocked in some way, and it only got worse as May blazed into June and Len's aura grew paler and paler, until it was like a small patch of fog fading in the sunlight.

Alice's aura had dipped into sickly greens in the days after receiving Oscar's message, but Edith was pleased to see that over time it had gained a richness, a deep emerald shimmering around the tangle of black hair and woollen cardigans that she wore in all weather. Edith did not know what happened to Oscar's head, and she did not know what Alice was doing to help her brother move on, but she seemed to be growing in some way, and that was something.

All seemed to be progressing well, until one evening in mid-June when Edith witnessed Len and Alice leave number four, turn out of the side gate, and make their way along the path to number two, where they knocked on the door and were admitted in a flurry of exclamations and cheek-kissing by Jackie Peach. Edith chewed on the biscuit she had just dunked in her lukewarm tea.

'Well, Frankie, this is new.'

Edith watched number two like a hawk and was finally rewarded when Len and Alice emerged just over an hour after entering. They returned to number four much more briskly than they had left it, and Edith cracked the window open to hear them arguing.

'...was a date! Mum just bloody left us and you're dating that horrible cow!'

'...not! Are you crazy? And don't derail this, you've never said anything about moving away next year!'

'Now who's derailing? Of course I'm moving away, I'm not staying here after school!'

Their auras were blazing, Len's a selection of blues, ice-white through to deepest navy, and Alice's rich orange and pink around dark purple. They entered number four at the side gate and a succession of slamming doors told Edith that the argument was not resolved when they got inside.

'Ah, my little Frankie mouse. It may be time for me to get involved.'

*

Alice and Len did not speak for the rest of the week. It was a fine day on Saturday and she had no wish to be in the house with her father, so Alice sat under the tree in the backyard and read a book. In between reading she would pause and look up at the forest over the back fence, thinking about her future. Her plan was to apply for university in the city and move in with her cousin, who she had been texting with over the last few weeks. This particular cousin was Fenella's niece, and Len's total silence on the sudden and apparently permanent absence of her mother had left Alice with the impression that he would not want his remaining child living with his estranged wife's side of the family. It was yet another conversation they had not had and it seemed to be one he was very sensitive about, judging by his reaction when she'd answered Jackie's polite enquiry about her plans after finishing school.

Despite not knowing her father's feelings on the topic of her mother's side of the family, Alice had gone ahead and done what was best for her, the lesson that Miss Greenhaven seemed to be teaching her. She thought about the conversation with her English teacher, when they had joked about cursing Chelsea Woodward. She pulled out her phone and searched simple revenge curses, immediately finding more than she could ever scroll through. She fixed on one at random. Most of the ingredients seemed easy to find and the procedure was simple enough. She put her book under her arm and started back inside.

'Psst!'

Alice looked around, panicked that Jackie Peach was trying to talk to her.

'Psst! Over here! By the gate!'

The voice was coming from the opposite side, where the alley cut between their house and Mrs Vanstone's. A small wizened face with large glasses strained to see her over the fence, and Alice approached. Mrs Vanstone seemed to be standing on something to see over the fence, but even that was not enough; her glasses bobbed up and down as she balanced on her toes. Alice opened the gate and helped the old woman off the stump she was teetering on.

'Oh good on you love, I wasn't holding on well up there.'

Alice stood back and waited for Mrs Vanstone to gather herself.

'Alright, now, you're here. Yes, I need to talk to you. I do, don't I? Yes, yes I need to talk to you little Alice.'

Alice bristled.

'I'm not little. What do you want Mrs Vanstone?'

Now Mrs Vanstone bristled.

'I'm not a Mrs, for God's sake! Call me Edith. I haven't been a Mrs for much longer than you've been alive, believe you me. No, Ms Vanstone to the bank manager and Edith to everyone else, except that damned Peach woman who can't keep more than one thing in her head at a time.' Edith muttered some expletives about Jackie and Alice's feelings towards her suddenly improved.

'Sorry. Edith. What's up, what you need to talk to me for?'

'Up, dear, the sky is up, as well I'm sure you know. No, there is nothing "up" that shouldn't be up, except perhaps your brother, but he is no longer up at all is he? In fact, he's rather quite down these days, six foot down I believe. Except for his head apparently, which must be a sorrow to the lad, rest his soul, wherever he is. No, I need to talk to you about the cats.'

Alice blinked, wondering how seriously to take this octogenarian. 'What cats?'

'The ones that come out in the evening, in this alley. I stopped feeding them about eight year ago so's you could do it, but I never said so and now I'm here telling you that I stopped feeding them and it's your responsibility now. Because that's what you do; you go out, do what needs doing, fix what needs fixing, and do the best you can with what you've got to work with, in this case cats, in my case gardening and hexes.'

'Gardening and... what? I have been feeding the cats, when I remember. What's that about hexes?'

'Oh bad business, bad it is. Don't go messing around with hexes and curses and whatnot, they work far better than they ever should and you regret it almost immediately, I can tell you from experience.'

Alice felt the weight of her phone in her hand, the curse she was just about to try lurking behind the lock screen.

'Listen. Don't ever forget feeding the cats, and don't put any curses on anyone as it's more trouble than it's worth and someone always gets hurt, usually not the one you were aiming for, 'specially when it comes to love, so don't go getting any ideas about such things. Let people fall in love or out of love as it pleases them 'cos it's difficult enough without another party getting involved, you just keep on keeping on and do what's best for you.'

Alice regarded her elderly neighbour, sorting through the convoluted message she was receiving and feeling none the wiser at the end of it. She smiled and shrugged.

'Ok. Feed the cats. Don't curse anyone. Got it.'

'I knew you'd understand. Smart girl. Always reading under trees and collecting the ends of life and caring for the beginnings of life.

That's the thing it is, that's the real thing about it all. They need help in the beginning and at the end, and it's only them in the middle who can help, and they're too busy leading their lives. Like my Derek, too busy being a lawyer or a doctor or whatever it is he does down in the city, never visits his old mum at the end of her life…' Edith had started walking away at the start of that sentence and by the time she was complaining about Derek she was at the end of the alley, nearly at her house. Alice watched her go, her arms crossed. She decided that Edith Vanstone was definitely a witch, although a different kind of witch to Miss Greenhaven, and went back to her tree to read instead of putting a curse on Chelsea Woodward or Jackie Peach.

The next day it rained prolifically, and once again the drain in front of the Morte house flooded, filling the cul-de-sac with the sweet-sour smell of their own waste. Len was at a nursery staring longingly at all the plants he didn't have time to take care of, so there was no one for Alice to complain to when she couldn't stand the stink that drifted under her reading tree. She surveyed the grey-brown flooding, which was advancing up the footpath to where she stood, and remembered her conversation with Edith.

You go out, do what needs doing, fix what needs fixing, and do the best you can with what you've got to work with.

What Alice had to work with was a pair of knee-high black wellies, a scarf long enough to tie over her nose, and a long-handled shovel. She changed into some old clothes put on a pair of swimming goggles to stop her eyes watering, and advanced on the smelly quagmire. She sloshed down the footpath and gingerly felt for the edge of the curb with her foot. Using the end of the shovel to find the opening of the drain, she prodded and probed around it, hoping to set something loose. Nothing happened. The water stayed stubbornly where it was, but she'd come this far and wasn't giving up without a fight, so she

kept probing, stirring up a slurry in unspeakable debris that had settled on the road.

After several minutes Len pulled into the cul-de-sac, having eventually purchased several packets of seeds that he would never plant.
He watched with surprise as his daughter attempted to fix the drain
that had become a manifestation of all his failures as a husband, father, and man. He pulled the van up to the edge of the flooded area.

'Allie! Any luck?'

She turned at the sound of her name and pulled the goggles off.
Her father was smiling, for the first time in what felt like forever.
Well, not smiling exactly, but his mouth twitched and his eyes
sparkled, his mask of stoicism cracked in the middle.

'Nope. It's pretty blocked.'

He laughed, rolled the window up, and drove the van through the
alley to park in the garage. Alice probed around a bit longer, still
thinking that through sheer force of will she could knock something
loose. Still nothing happened, and she gave up, not wanting flood water and sewage to tip into her boots. She rinsed off in the back yard,
returned the spade to the greenhouse, and went upstairs for a long
hot shower. By the time she came back down to the kitchen Len had
finally come in from the garage, with puffy eyes and a croaky voice
that betrayed him. Alice was relieved that he hadn't cried in front of
her, although she would have stayed with him if he had. As it was,
she gave him a big hug while he was making tea, unblocking their
relationship of the festering silence that had been there since it was
just the two of them.

Part IV:
Absence &
Absolution

IV

Absence & Absolution

The 31st of July was Alice's 17th birthday and the first one in her whole life that she didn't have to share with Oscar. All she could think of all day was that Oscar was always going to be 16 and every year she would continue to grow older than him, and even though he was the worst, that really was very sad. She had resolved not to make first contact with her mother on the day, and without thinking about it too much she knew that it was a test. She was relieved to the point of tears when Fenella sent her a message mid-afternoon, saying:

"Hi Allie, happy birthday!! How are things?"

To which Alice replied:

"Hi Mum. Things r ok I guess. Oscar's still dead. You're still gone. That drain keeps flooding. Jackie still sucks. But Dad's a bit better."

And almost a second after sending it she received a wall of text, which Fenella must have been typing while Alice was replying to her first message.

"Darling I want you to know that I didn't leave because of you. I am sorry I left, but things just aren't the same and being in the house is so sad for me. I was never really sure I wanted a family and the years I spent with your father feel like such a waste now that I'm off on my own after so much time. You're old enough to understand these things now so..."

The message went on in similar fashion, but Alice didn't finish reading it. She considered throwing her phone out the window, then received another message from Fenella:

'I've spoken to someone I know at the council about the flooding problem. They're sending people to fix it next week. Happy birthday.'

Alice flopped back on her bed and turned her music up.

'Thanks Mum.'

*

Alice couldn't pinpoint the date when Oscar's voice stopped whispering in her ear while she was at number four Yardley Court, but she realised in mid-August, the day that the council workers unblocked the drain, that she hadn't heard from Oscar clearly since before their birthday. The only reason she was thinking about him at all on that day was because when the drain was excavated it was discovered that the cause of the blockage was a human skull, approximately the size of that of a teenage boy. Alice and Edith had been watching the council workers from their respective windows in their respective houses, and Edith felt a small jolt when she realised that the lumpy grey thing that was being disentangled from sticks and leaves was a human skull. She ran to her Ouija board and was greeted with an energetic buzzing that translated to 'ZZZZZZZZZZZZZ' on the board. She knew for sure then that the skull was Oscar's.

She ran down the stairs, intending to knock on the Morte's door and tell them what she had seen, but by the time she opened her front door Alice and Len were already out there, examining the grisly find. Edith kept the door open a crack, straining to hear what was being said.

'Coo-ee! Alice, sweetheart! And Len, dear! Finally getting that drain fixed I see!'

Both Len and Alice looked up like startled deer at Jackie's voice. She was getting out of her car on the edge of the cul-de-sac, carrying several shopping bags.

'Oh, uh, yeah, glad to finally get it done. Here let me help with that Jacks,' Len almost ran to her, grabbing some of the bags and spinning her around like a top so she didn't see what had been found in the drain. Len was no fool; he knew Jackie would get mileage out of this for months and there was no way he was going through that again.

Edith later heard that the skull was identified by its teeth as definitely being Oscar's, although they were chipped and cracked from being clenched so hard. She spent some time visualising what she had witnessed that day back in October, wondering how on earth the boy's head had separated from his body, moved the distance across the road to the drain, and then tumbled down it. It made no sense, and as Oscar had spent the better part of his first year being dead seeking his head from the other side she doubted he knew how it got there either, so in the end she chalked it up to remaining one of life's great mysteries.

*

Alice and Edith only had one more conversation that year, again in the alley between their houses. Alice explained in a monotone with an edge of morbid amusement that Oscar's head had been extracted from the drain and identified by its teeth, and Edith listened and nodded with an appropriate look of horror on her face. While they were talking Len wandered past with a barrow full of compost and said a hearty hello, continuing on his way to the front garden.

'He seems much happier your dad, much happier than he has been, and that's since his son's head was, as you just told me, extracted from the drain in front of your house.'

'Uh, yeah... I think he's a bit better. He really doesn't want me to leave next year. I'm worried about him on his own, that Jackie Peach will... you know. Get her way.'

Edith thought for a moment, her eyes glazed behind her large glasses.

'What is it that your dad likes most in the world? What does he want to do? Does he like being a plumber? Is it his calling?'

'Umm, no I don't think so. I don't know. He doesn't hate it. But he does love gardening. He doesn't get much time for it. He said if he won the lottery he'd semi-retire, sell the business but keep a few days on-call or something, then spend the rest of the time growing things.'

Edith continued to look thoughtful. Alice laughed softly, remembering.

'He built that greenhouse when me and Oscar were five and we've only ever used it to keep all our crap in. I think if he could semi-retire he'd turn it into the best greenhouse ever.'

Edith looked her hard in the eye, which felt like making eye contact with a dazed guppy, and said suddenly, 'Jackie has an electrician.'

Alice, who was becoming accustomed to the way conversations with Edith tended to jump all over the place, simply nodded as though she knew what this meant. Edith continued.

'An electrician. Hm. Yes. How often does one need an electrician do you think? Once a month? Once a year? How about every Thursday night from eight to nine? What do you think needs doing from eight to nine o'clock every Thursday evening?'

Alice's eyes widened. Surely Edith wasn't saying...

'And I'm not a gossip. I'm sure it's something electrical this electrician does for Jackie. And I'm sure his wedding ring helps with it too, whatever it is. This electrical thing.'

Alice waited for a wink, but perhaps she missed it behind the distorting effect of the glasses. Her implication stretched to breaking point, Edith returned to normal, or as normal as she could go.

'Now, I see you been feeding the cats. Good. That's good. I got something else for you to feed, although as he's no longer technic'ly a living thing I don't think he should be eating, but he is, so I suppose that's that.'

She reached into the woollen sleeve of her jumper and pulled out little Frankie, who had been snug and warm and asleep and was not happy to be woken up and handed to a startled teenager. Alice held him gently in her palm, looking closely at him.

'What do you mean 'not a living entity'?'

'Never you mind, just keep him away from Oulie and power outlets and you'll be fine.'

'Why are you giving him to me? Are you going away?'

Edith did not answer at first, just looked blankly at Frankie.

'We always know, you know. It's a... thing. That we have. Part of the Sight. We can see what's coming, even if it's shit. And I can't prevent this shit. It'll hit the proverbial fan and that'll be that. Or my proverbial fan. I forget the saying.'

Alice again nodded as though she understood. Edith started to walk away; it seemed their meeting was at an end.

'And don't forget the cats!'

*

Alice took Frankie to school with her for the rest of the year, carrying him around in her sleeve or the front pocket on her hoodie. He mainly slept, occasionally emerging for crumbs and scraps of paper. Miss Greenhaven took a liking to him, which gave Alice an idea.

She didn't immediately tell Miss Greenhaven that her brother's head had been found stuck down the drain in front of her house. Partly she was worried her teacher wouldn't believe her, and partly she didn't want Miss Greenhaven to take this as a sign that she didn't need to come to her office every lunch time. But after Edith bequeathed Frankie to her, and after she saw how tenderly Miss Greenhaven fed and patted him, she decided it was time to take a risk.

'I don't feel haunted anymore.'

'Mm?'

'I think Oscar's at peace now.'

'That's good.'

'They found his head.'

Miss Greenhaven looked at her with raised eyebrows, holding a piece of paper for Frankie to nibble.

'It was stuck in the drain in front of our house. So I guess it wasn't disintegrated. No one knows how it got in there. It's definitely his head. It was buried with him on the weekend. They got special permission to dig up his coffin and...' Alice trailed off with a shrug.

'Well... that's good. You know, I thought when you said you were being haunted that it was a metaphor. Like, you were grieving and felt haunted by losing him.'

'I didn't lose him. Only his head. But that's found again now. And it was a metaphor. I think. I don't know.'

They were silent for a moment.

'I've been thinking about what I'm going to study next year.'

'Oh?'

'I want to be a teacher.'

Miss Greenhaven barked out a laugh, sending Frankie skittering into her pencil case.

'Oh, I'm sorry Frankie, I didn't mean to scare you.' She coaxed him out, then frowned at Alice.

'That's a terrible idea. Being a teacher is awful. You should do something much more valuable and rewarding.'

'I think I'd be a good teacher. I'd let sad, pathetic kids hang out in my office, I'd give them books, I'd-'

'No. Alice, you are an exception. I would never do this for anyone. I hate most of my students. To be a teacher you have to be like a soldier, shooting people with knowledge even as you're sinking into the mud, crying out for death. It's not fun, it's not easy, and only a few people last long enough to become properly inspirational, magnanimous, life-saving fonts of knowledge like Michelle Pfeiffer in that movie. Or Hilary Swank in that other movie.'

'Or Robin Williams in that other movie?'

'Exactly. Movies make being a teacher look easy. Or at least regularly rewarding. I think you should do what everyone else does and have teaching as your back up.'

'Shouldn't you be encouraging me to follow my dreams, wherever they may take me? And persevere with something even if it's difficult?'

'Maybe if this were a movie. Following your dream and pursuing a career, or even just holding down a job, are not the same thing. Find something that you can stand, in an environment that won't kill your spirit, with enough variety that you want to keep going there, year after year, and do that.'

Alice chewed on her thumbnail, feeling hurt. Miss Greenhaven could not be flattered, but she thought she'd at least be pleased that Alice wanted to be like her.

'So if you hate teaching so much then what's your dream?'

'I didn't say I hate teaching, I said I hate my students.

'So you like teaching?'

'I like knowing things that other people don't know, and I like bossing people around, and I like having a regular routine with scheduled time off. I knew I'd hating working in an office with the same people all day, every day. I knew I couldn't do something soul-destroying like advertising or banking or selling insurance. I knew that I'd probably murder someone if I was an air hostess.'

Alice snorted, imagining Miss Greenhaven in a neat uniform serving drinks.

'So I narrowed it down, and this seemed like my best bet. And it's worked out pretty well.'

'I don't know what I like. Or what I don't like.'

'Yes you do. Or if you don't, you'll figure it out pretty quick. If you can survive being haunted by your dead twin brother you can do anything. There you go, that was inspirational wasn't it?'

Part V.
Death &
Departure

V

Death & Departure

That October, the first anniversary of Oscar's death and a few weeks before exams, Alice was studying in her room when she heard a knock at the front door. She came downstairs, out the side door and through the greenhouse to the front porch, where stood Jackie Peach in the smallest dress with the biggest hair Alice had ever seen.

'The door's still broken,' she said when Jackie knocked again, not noticing her come out the side gate.

'Oh! Oh, I'm sorry sweetheart, I thought your father had fixed it. He's such a clever man!'

'What do you want?'

'I, oh, well I had actually hoped to talk to Len. I thought he was home and you'd still be at school. Having a sick day are we?'

'Studying. Why do you need to talk to him?'

'Oh sweetie, it's about adult things I'm afraid. I'll just wait until he's home and come in the side gate-'

'What adult things?'

'Oh, um, I, just need his help. With a drain. I have my own clogged drain. As a plumber I thought he could give me a hand. Or two.'

Alice crossed her arms and looked Jackie up and down, taking in every inch of her from head to toe.

'So... a regular visit from an electrician isn't enough is it? You need a free plumber as well?'

'I-what? Look sweetie, I'm sure-'

'I can't imagine what you need fixing on Thursday night every week from eight to nine. You'll have to start a schedule: electrician on Thursdays, plumber on Tuesdays.'

Alice looked her dead in the eye and didn't blink, and Jackie's long doll-lashes fluttered with fury.

'I have a dodgy oven.'

'Well, careful there's no buns in it or his wife might get upset.'

It took every ounce of Alice's self-control not to smirk at her terribly clever joke, and she continued staring Jackie in the eye.

Jackie audibly gasped, putting a manicured hand to her well-moulded bosom. She huffed, opening and closing her mouth, but nothing came out.

'Leave my dad alone. He needs peace and quiet. If he's ever interested in you, I'm sure he'll let you know.'

Jackie took a step backward, teetering in sky-high heels, then turned unsteadily and stomped back to her own house. Alice wondered where she kept her keys in that ensemble.

She didn't tell her father about what happened with Jackie, but she did say that someone had knocked on the front door again thinking it was working. Len ate his mashed potato thoughtfully.

'Can you give me a hand with it on Saturday?'

*

That weekend Alice and Len Morte cleaned out everything of Oscar's and Fenella's from the house and the greenhouse. Fenella's boxes and suitcases, which had never been picked up by the courier, were sent to her sister's place on the other side of the country, where they presumed she was staying. Oscar's bicycles, sports equipment, clothes, magazines, and old toys were donated to a charity, although Len kept behind a few things in a box that he put under his bed. They then went to the hardware store and bought everything they needed to fix the front door.

Neither of them used the new door even after it was fixed, and Len never patched the burnt parts of the wall or the kitchen window. Alice was pleased by this. The charred front of the house was a part of their history as a family of two, and some scars, although they heal, should be kept as reminders of what one has endured.

Alice sat her exams in November, achieving high marks in all subjects, which she was very pleased with, not least of all because she achieved much higher marks than Chelsea Woodward and the rest of the Witches' Guild members.

On her last day at school she visited Miss Greenhaven in her office and bequeathed Frankie to her, as she was not sure she'd be able to look after him when she moved away. She told Miss Greenhaven that she was not going to be a teacher, even though she knew she'd be great at it, but that she had recently discovered a talent for asking difficult questions and holding her nerve under pressure, and that she was thinking of becoming a journalist. Miss Greenhaven, who was not the least bit religious, crossed herself and said, 'May God have mercy on our souls.'

The weekend after her exams finished, Alice knocked on Edith's door to tell her that Frankie had gone up in the world. She was startled when it was opened by a woman she vaguely recognised as Margaret, Edith's carer who came twice a week. Margaret gently told Alice that Edith had passed away in the night, and by all accounts it seemed to have been peaceful and without pain. Alice nodded, then returned home, where she opened a new can of cat food and fed it to the strays on the edge of the forest. She cried for several minutes, telling the cats of Edith's passing. They didn't seem to care, but they happily ate all the food.

Some time later, Alice and Len received a visit from a woman in a suit who turned out to be the executor of Edith's estate. It seemed that she had left her house and all its contents to 'the remaining Mortes, at number four.' Len and Alice, sitting at the table with the suited woman, thought it was a mistake. But the solicitor showed them the will and the letter Edith had written several months before, which stated that she had no real care for the house and it wasn't worth that much, but that she hoped it would let the Mortes follow their dreams. And there was also a reminder about feeding the stray cats of the neighbourhood, plus a small stipend for someone to clean up the rubbish in the forest behind the cul-de-sac. So it was that the week before she was due to move to the city and live with her cousin, Alice and her father spent several days cleaning out Edith's house. They tried repeatedly to contact Derek, but he never replied to them, so they let him be.

While they were cleaning Edith's study upstairs Alice found shelves and shelves of books on witchcraft, herb gardens, and developing one's psychic abilities. She flipped through a few of them, kept the gardening ones for Len, and donated the rest. She had come to the conclusion, after much reflection, that she did not believe in witches, or the supernatural, or even spirits. In the year since Oscar died Miss Greenhaven had taught her that sometimes it takes the right person in the right place at the right time to make a real difference, and that most things really can't be controlled. Edith had taught her to do what needs doing, fix what needs fixing, and do what you can with what you've got to work with, and that that can be controlled, but it's entirely up to you. And Jackie Peach had taught her that some people are basically fetid rodents, even if they have really good hair. She kept one of Edith's witchcraft books, on practical revenge curses, just for memory's sake.

With the greenhouse cleared out Len was able to start growing things in it, and with the extra income from renting out number six Yardley Court he was able to sell his plumbing business and semi-retire. Jebediah, the elderly gentleman who rented Edith's old house, was a retired professor of botany. He was grateful for the quiet of the suburbs, the forest nearby, and, over time, the pleasure of Len's company, whom he regularly helped with his gardening projects. Jebediah also liked to take long walks in the forest behind the cul-de-sac, but he never discovered Edith's lettuce patch, more's the pity, and it went to seed and eventually died off without her to care for it.

Before Alice left for the city she put a curse on Jackie Peach. She no longer believed in such things – she attributed Oscar's whispers from the other side to the trauma and grief of losing two family members in six months – but she was worried that when she left number four Yardley Court Jackie would resume her pursuit of Len, and thought that cursing their neighbour would make herself feel better about it all. So she gathered the required ingredients, most of which she found in Edith's ailing kitchen garden, undertook the rites, and cursed Jackie with the rather tame malady of becoming tongue-tied whenever she was near Len.

Alice never knew it, but the curse worked perfectly, to the point where if Jackie was within shouting distance of Len she could barely open her mouth. As number two and number four were quite close to each other, this had the effect of rendering Jackie speechless in half of her house, and over time it made her more thoughtful and self-aware. Although not that much; she still loved to phone people and gossip, she'd just do it from the other side of her house.

Oulie, who was staring down the barrel of canine middle-age, did not take well to being ousted from the greenhouse when Alice and

Len cleared it out. He would howl in the backyard, refuse to get into his kennel, then refuse to come out of it. He went off his food, and wouldn't even chase sheep on the farms on the other side of the forest any more. Finally, Len relented, and moved his kennel back into the greenhouse, where he was much happier.

*

Oulie always wondered, in his black and white dog brain, what happened to his master. One minute he was feeling nervous as the thunder grew closer, barking up at the roof where his master was perched like a pesky crow, and the next minute he was on the ground, smelling funny, not waking up. Oulie, being the good dog he was, knew that something was wrong and nudged Oscar, nuzzling his arms, his head. When he didn't move and no one was coming to help, Oulie took evasive action, grasping Oscar's ear in his teeth and pulling, pulling him towards home and help. Oscar's neck, brittle and broken from the lightning and the two-storey drop, could not withstand the tugging of an insistent golden retriever, and gave way. It rolled and bumped and tumbled towards home, never quite reaching it, but slipping down the drain, where it would remain for many months. Oulie knew then that his master was gone, although it was difficult for him to understand, and he wandered off into the forest to chase cats and roll in the funny-smelling patch of scratchy plants.

The End.

ACKNOWLEDGEMENTS

I'd like to say thank you to all the people who have been there cheering me on through the journey of my becoming a real-and-proper writer.

My husband, for always supporting and cheering on my myriad interests, which are often bumping into each other and getting in the way of everyday life.

My parents, for fostering a deep love of literature and learning, and for generally discouraging conformity.

My brother, for all the fun, interesting conversations that would make no sense to anyone else.

My wider family – grandparents, aunts, uncles, cousins – who I haven't seen in a long time but have always been receptive and indulgent to an oddball little girl who is interested in everything – taking me on trips to widen my horizons and giving me beautiful, thoughtful gifts to keep me crafting, even from across the country.

The Underground Writers team, for always being willing to try my ideas, even when they're still coming to terms with my last idea.

My writing friends, for being accepting, receptive and supportive, no matter how specific or outlandish my questions.

And my cat, whose random ankle-biting gives me daily adrenaline.

Jemimah is an LGBT+ Australian writer, reader and editor who has been published in The Big Issue, ArtsHub, the Planet Bastard anthology, Invisible Ink's *Trace* anthology, and on several blogs. She sits on Aurealis Award judging panels and writes short fiction, book reviews, blog posts, and a fortnightly newsletter called The Brew.

In between writing and reading she watches a lot of cosy television, drinks bucketloads of tea, and rides her motorbike.

www.ingramcontent.com/pod-product-compliance
Lightning Source LLC
Chambersburg PA
CBHW020236120726
47903CB00008B/2693